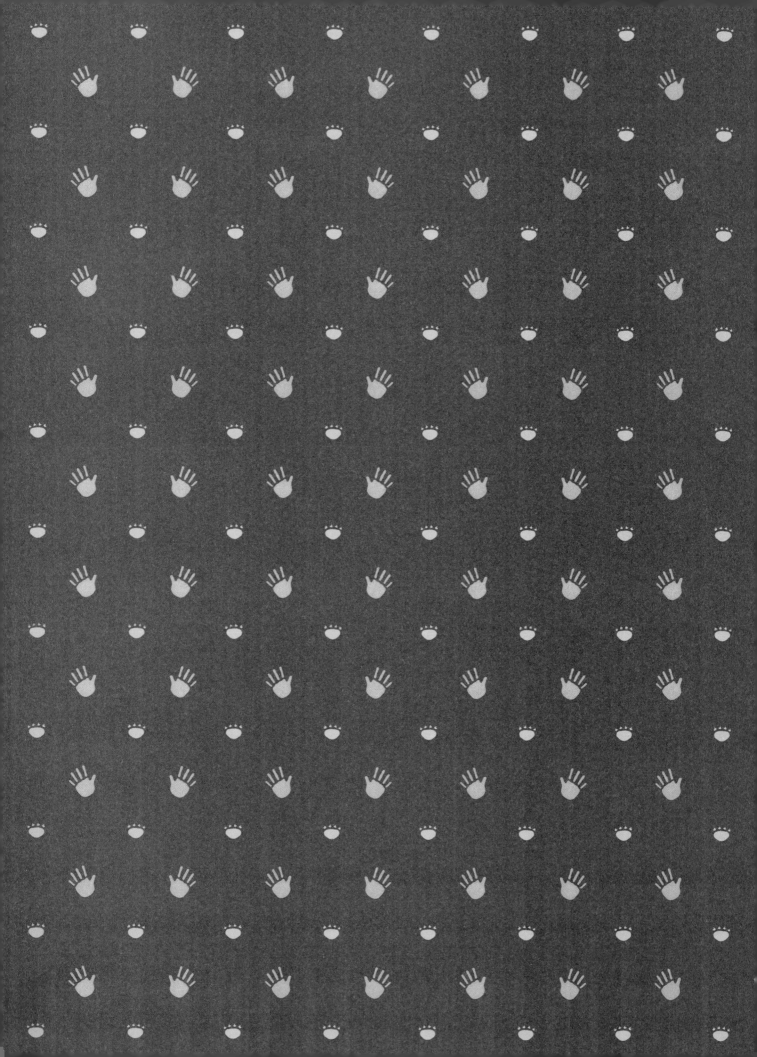

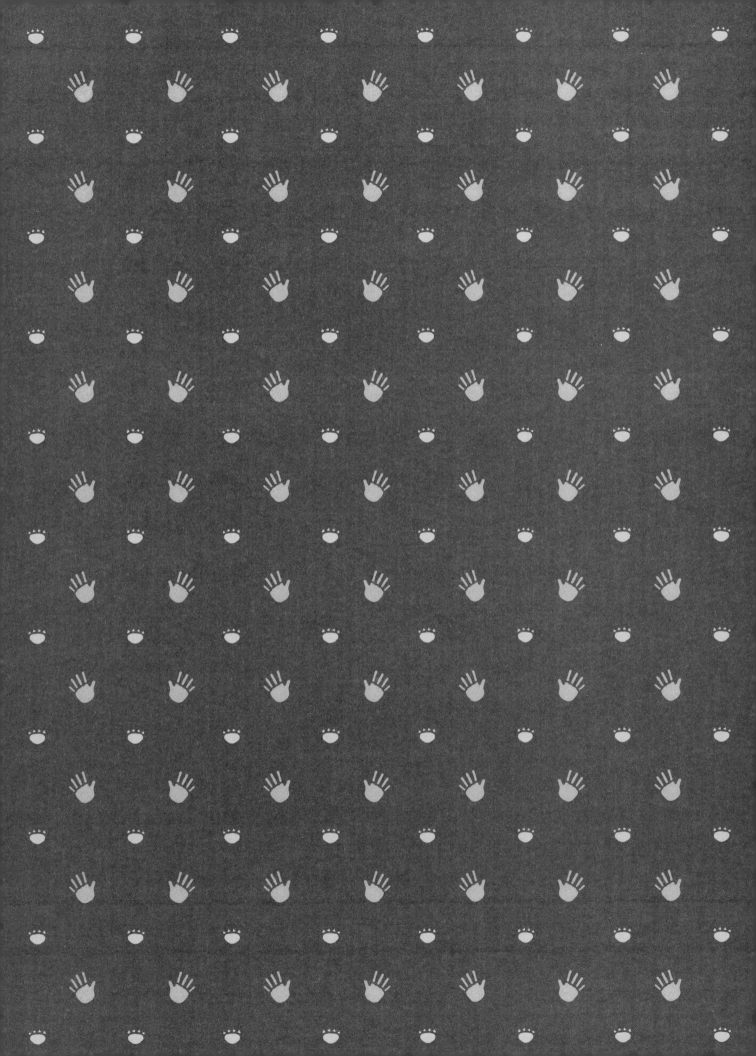

To my niece Natalie — B.C.

ISBN 0-590-25488-X

Text copyright © 1994 by Paulette Bourgeois.
Illustrations copyright © 1994 by Brenda Clark.
All rights reserved. Published by Scholastic Inc., 555 Broadway, New York, NY 10012, by arrangement with Kids Can Press Ltd.

24 23 22 21 20 19 18   9/9 0 1 2 3/0

Printed in U.S.A.   14

First Scholastic printing, April 1995

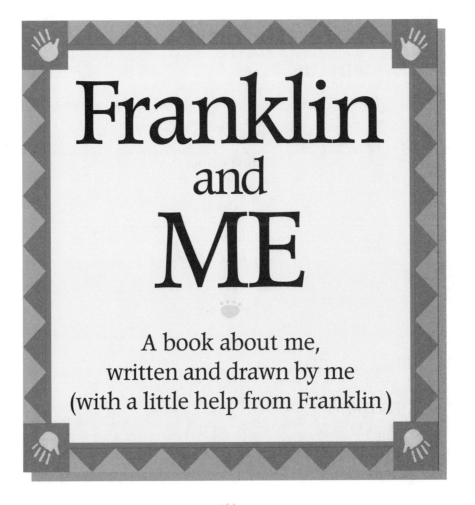

Franklin
and
ME

A book about me,
written and drawn by me
(with a little help from Franklin)

Written by Paulette Bourgeois

Illustrated by Brenda Clark

SCHOLASTIC INC.

New York   Toronto   London   Auckland   Sydney

★ Franklin and Me ★

This is a book about me!

My name is: _____
first name

_____
middle name

_____
last name

I got my name because:

☐ it's a great name

☐ I am named after a famous person

☐ I am named after a parent or grandparent

☐ I am named after
someone special named _____

I started making this book on

_____ ,
month   day   year

when I was _____ years old.

This is Franklin.

This is me.

Draw a picture or put a photo of yourself here.

Franklin was named after a character in a television show called *M*A*S*H*. The man, named Benjamin Franklin Pierce, was afraid of dark places.

★ When I Was a Baby ★

Here is my baby picture.

✏️ I was born on

_____
month

_____
day

_____
year

at _____.
time

Put your baby photo here.

✏️ I was born: ☐ at home   ☐ in a car   ☐ in a hospital

✏️ I was born in _____
village, town or city

in _____.
country

✏️ I weighed _____ and was _____ long.

★ When I Was Little ★

I took my first step when I was _____ old.

I got my first tooth when I was _____ old.

My first word was _____.

I got my first haircut when I was _____ old.

Franklin got his favorite cuddly blanket when he was little.

Circle the cuddly things you like.

 Draw a picture of your favorite cuddly thing here.

★ This Is Me Now! ★

My hair is this color:

- [ ] red
- [ ] black
- [ ] purple
- [ ] brown
- [ ] yellow
- [ ] green
- [ ] white
- [ ] striped

My hair is:

- [ ] curly
- [ ] straight
- [ ] short
- [ ] long
- [ ] wavy

My face looks like this.

Draw a picture of your face here.

My eyes are this color.
Use a crayon to color these eyes.

Franklin has spots on
his head. Count the spots!

✎ I have freckles:

☐ on my nose

☐ all over my face

☐ all over my arms

☐ all over my body

☐ nowhere

Count your freckles!

✎ My belly button: ☐ sticks out ☐ pokes in

✎ My knees have: ☐ no scrapes ☐ lots of scrapes

✎ ☐ I wear glasses. ☐ I do not wear glasses.

✎ ☐ I use a wheelchair. ☐ I do not use a wheelchair.

✎ ☐ I have broken a bone. ☐ I have never broken a bone.

✎ ☐ I have had stitches. ☐ I have never had stitches.

★ My Hands and Feet ★

Did you know that nobody else in the whole world has fingerprints just like yours?

This is my hand.

Ask an adult to help you make a print of your hand,
using paint or a stamp pad.

This is Franklin's footprint.

I wear boots and shoes like this:

Circle the ones you wear.

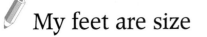 My feet are size

_____.

My foot looks like this.

 Ask an adult to help you draw around your foot.

My Family

This is Franklin's family.

This is my family.

Draw a picture or put a photo of your family here.

✏️ The names of the people in my family are:

_____   _____

_____   _____

_____   _____

✏️ These people are my relatives:

_____   _____

_____   _____

✏️ I am: ☐ the oldest child ☐ the youngest child
☐ in the middle ☐ the only child ☐ a twin

✏️ The language my
family speaks at home is _____.

✏️ My favorite family
celebration is called _____.

✏️ My favorite
family activity is _____.

★ My Home ★

This is Franklin's room.

Follow his footprints to find a picture of his home.

Look along the bottom of the page. Can you find a home that looks like yours?

My home is made of: ☐ brick ☐ wood ☐ straw ☐ cement ☐ stone ☐ gingerbread

My favorite room at home is _____.

I like it best because _____.

My room looks like this.

Draw a picture of your room.

My room is: ☐ tidy ☐ messy ☐ a little bit of both

☐ I share my room with _____.

☐ I do not share my room.

★ My Friends ★

These are Franklin's friends.

Franklin likes to play with his friends.

These are the things I like to do with my friends:

Circle the things you like to do.

do a puzzle

play ball

skip

play tag

play marbles

swim

play school

play dolls

play house

build

skate

play hide and seek

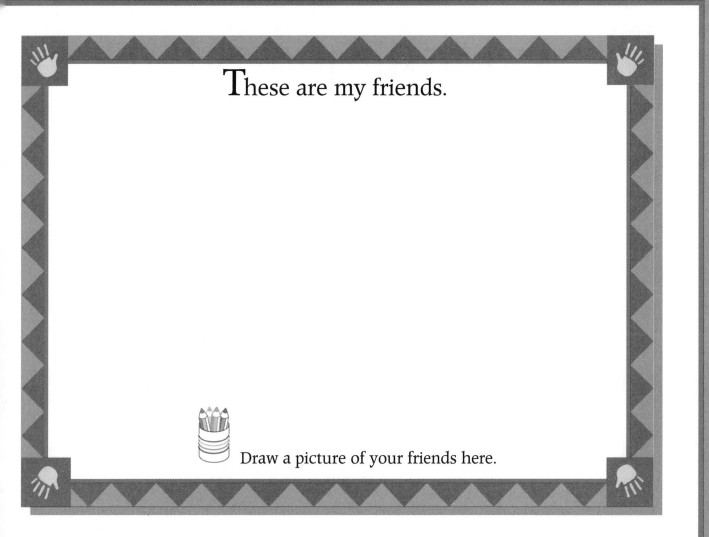

These are my friends.

Draw a picture of your friends here.

✎ The names of my friends are:

_____   _____

_____   _____

Franklin likes to play by himself too.

✎ When I am alone
I like to _____.

★ My Neighborhood ★

_____

number and street

_____

town

_____

city

_____

country

_____

zip code

_____

phone number

These are some of the people I know in my neighborhood:

Circle the people you know.

neighbor	doctor	crossing guard
police officer	dentist	babysitter
garbage collector	fire fighter	librarian
store clerk	mail carrier	mechanic

These are some of the things I see in my neighborhood:

Circle the things you see.

★ My Doctor ★

✏ My doctor's name is _____.

My doctor helps to keep me healthy and cares for me if I feel sick.

✏ My doctor says I am

_____ tall
how tall?

and weigh _____.
how much?

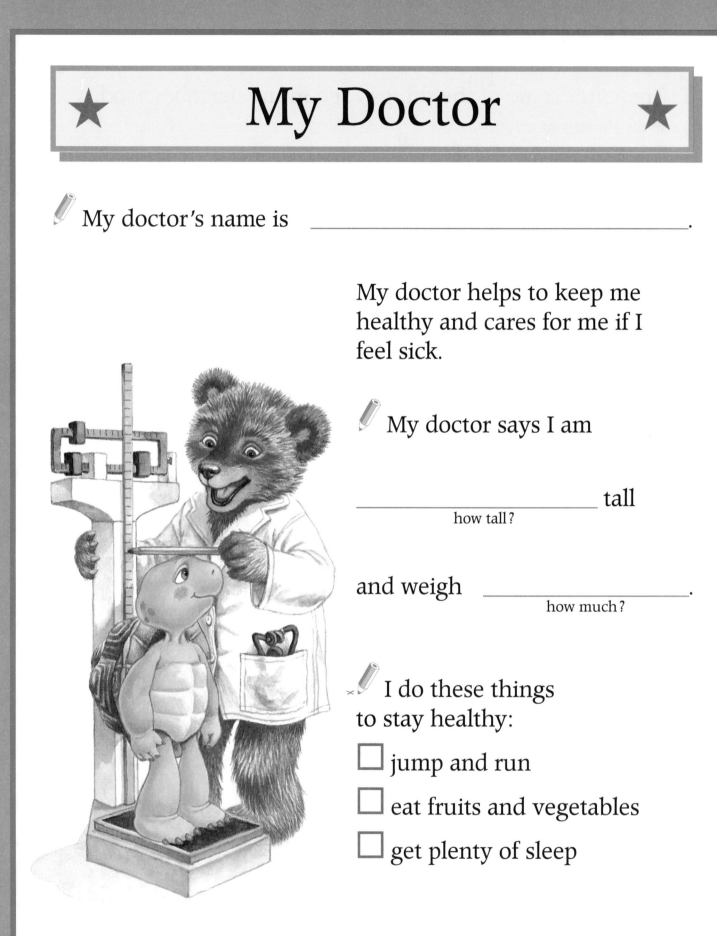

✏ I do these things to stay healthy:

☐ jump and run

☐ eat fruits and vegetables

☐ get plenty of sleep

My Dentist

My dentist's name is _____.

My dentist helps to keep my teeth healthy.

I visit
my dentist _____ times a year.
_{how many?}

I brush
my teeth _____ times a day.
_{how many?}

I have _____ teeth.
_{how many?}

I have _____ wiggly teeth.
_{how many?}

I have lost _____ teeth.
_{how many?}

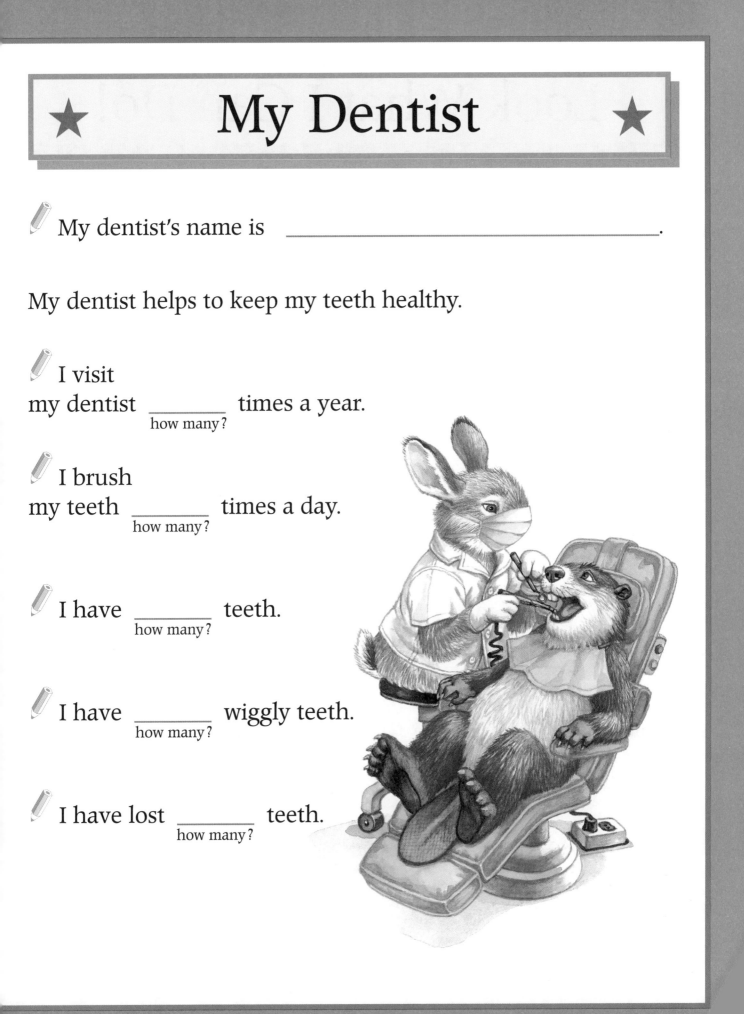

★ Look What I Can Do! ★

Franklin can do these things:

I can do these things too:

☐ tie shoes

☐ count by twos

☐ button buttons

☐ zip zippers

☐ count forwards and backwards

I am learning to:

Circle the things you are learning to do.

read	print	count
skate	tell time	do backwards somersaults
ride a bicycle	swim	make music

I am also learning to _____

_____.

The thing I do best is _____

_____.

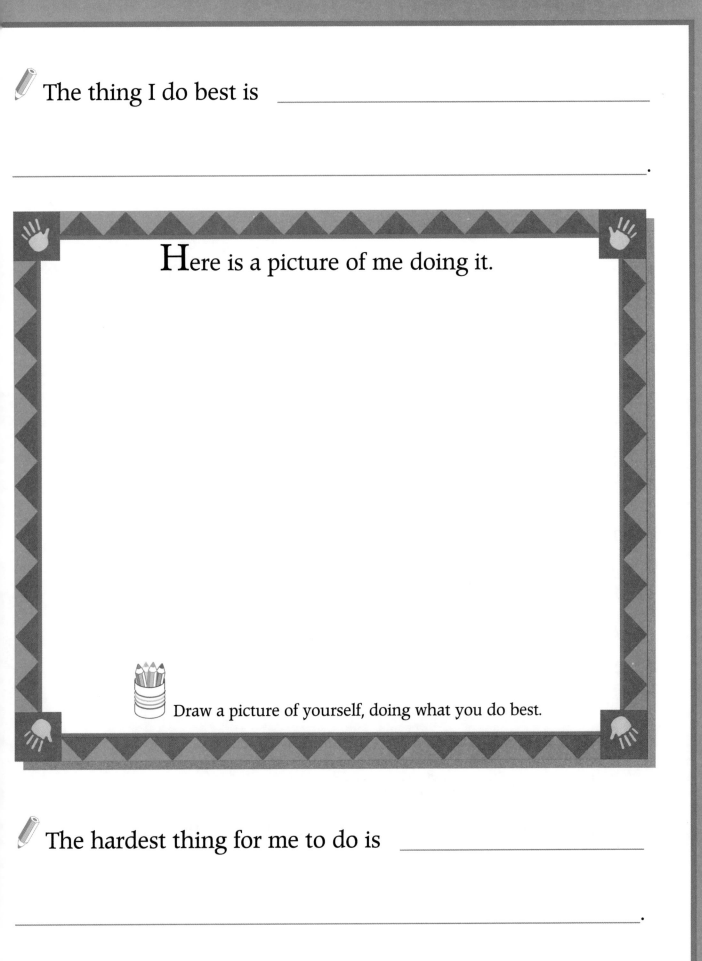

Here is a picture of me doing it.

Draw a picture of yourself, doing what you do best.

The hardest thing for me to do is _____

_____.

★ Me Around the Clock ★

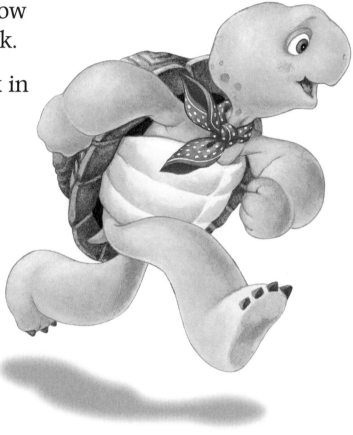

When Franklin wants to know the time, he looks at the clock.

His wake-up time is 7 o'clock in the morning.

His lunch time is 12 o'clock noon.

His supper time is 6 o'clock.

His bedtime is 7 o'clock at night.

Franklin's favorite time of the day is 4 o'clock. That's snack time!

My favorite time of the day is _____.

Franklin's mother tells him to "Hurry up."

☐ I am always ready on time.

☐ I am never ready on time – unless it's time for a party.

☐ Sometimes I have to hurry up, when _____.

This is what the clock says when:

Draw the hands on each clock.

I wake up.

I eat lunch.

I eat supper.

I go to bed at night.

Good night, Franklin!

My School

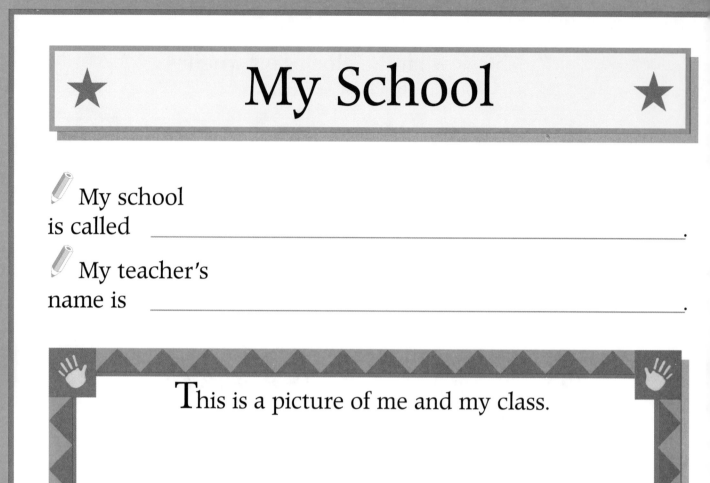

My school is called _____.

My teacher's name is _____.

This is a picture of me and my class.

Draw a picture or put a photo of your class here.

This is what we do at school:

Circle the things you do at school.

read books	build	water play
tell stories	play outside	cook
show and tell	sing	write stories
draw	share snacks	count
play instruments	paint	measure

What I like most about school is _____

_____.

My class went on a trip to _____

_____.

★ My Favorites ★

Franklin likes fly pie,
baseball,
hide and seek,
his blue blanket,
his night light and
the color purple.

I have lots of
favorite things.

 My favorite
book is _____.

 My favorite
game is _____.

 My favorite
color is _____.

 Fill in the square with
your favorite color.

These are my favorite foods.

Draw a picture of your favorite foods.

My favorite
sport is _____.

My favorite
toys are _____.

My favorite
animal is _____.

Places I Go

★ ★

Franklin goes to the riverbank to play and goes into the berry patch with his friend Bear.

He visits his father's friend Mole.

I like to visit _____.

I have been to visit these places : Circle the places you have visited.

zoo   library   park   fire station

farm   beach   airport   museum

I have traveled by:

☐ car   ☐ train   ☐ boat   ☐ airplane

☐ subway   ☐ bus   ☐ camel

★ More About Me ★

Franklin has a pet goldfish.

✏️ ☐ I have a pet. It is a _____

and it is called _____.

✏️ ☐ I do not have a pet. But if I had one it would be a:
Circle the pet you would like.

fish   cat   bird   horse

dog   rabbit   lizard   hippopotamus

and I would call it _____.

✏️ I collect: ☐ coins   ☐ dolls   ☐ stickers
☐ stamps   ☐ bottle caps

☐ something else: _____

★ My Feelings ★

Franklin was happy when he won a race.

He was afraid when he was lost in the woods.

He was worried when he told a fib.

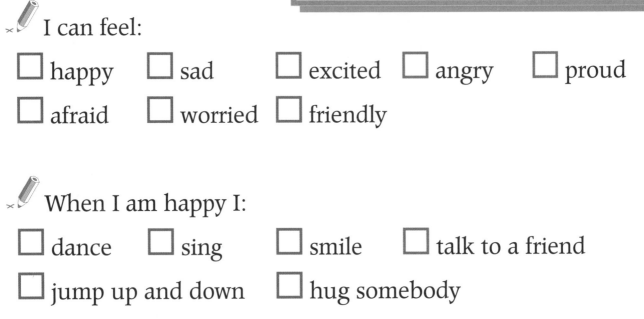

I can feel:

☐ happy   ☐ sad   ☐ excited   ☐ angry   ☐ proud

☐ afraid   ☐ worried   ☐ friendly

When I am happy I:

☐ dance   ☐ sing   ☐ smile   ☐ talk to a friend

☐ jump up and down   ☐ hug somebody

More feelings.

Find pictures that show feelings and put them here. Look in old magazines, draw pictures or use photos of people you know.

My Party

Happy Birthday!

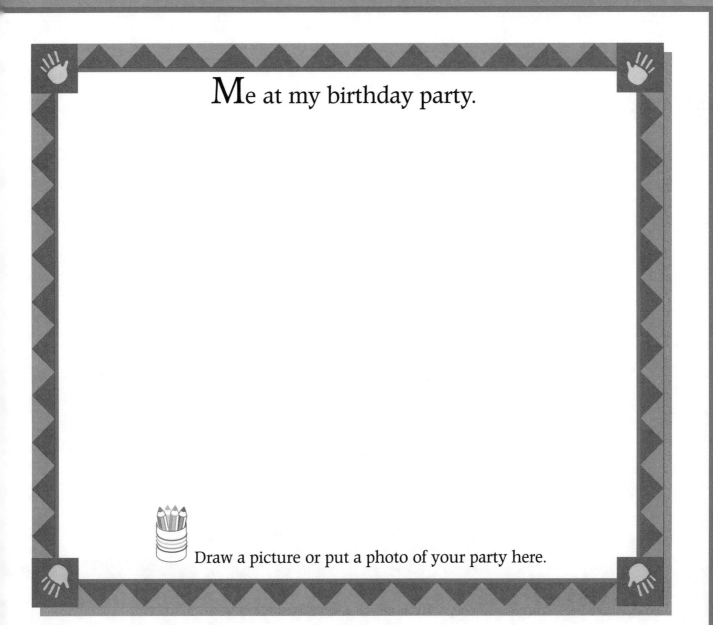

Me at my birthday party.

Draw a picture or put a photo of your party here.

✏️ There were _____ candles on my cake.
how many?

✏️ At my party
we ate _____.

✏️ At my party
we played _____.

✏️ The most special thing
about my party was _____.

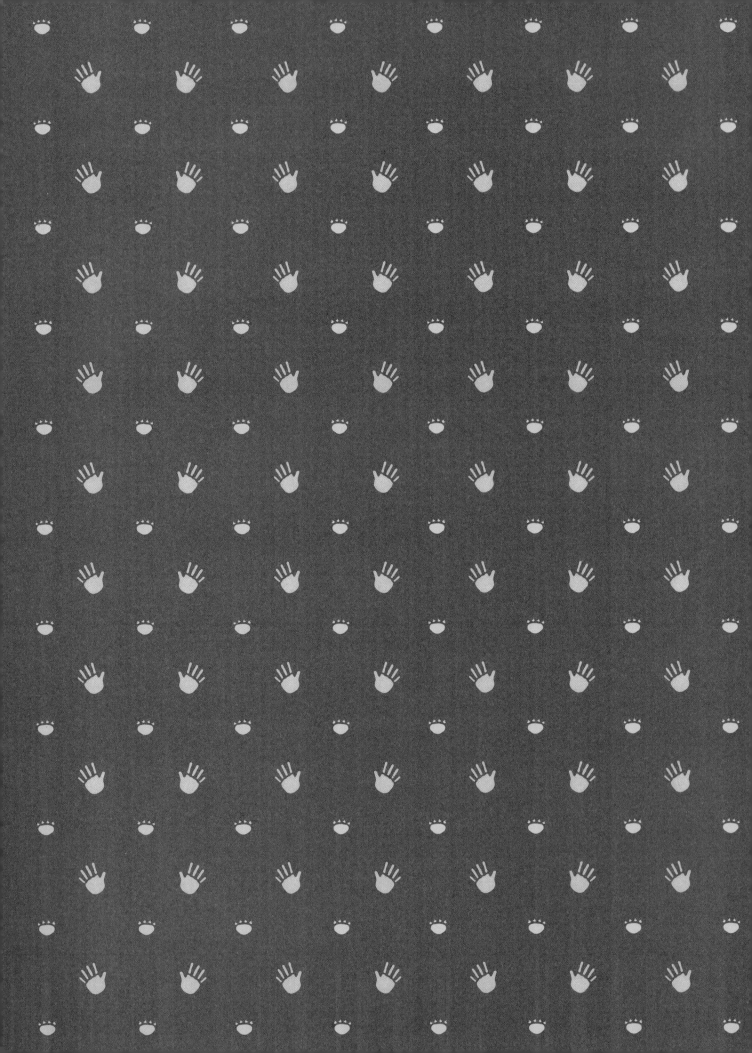

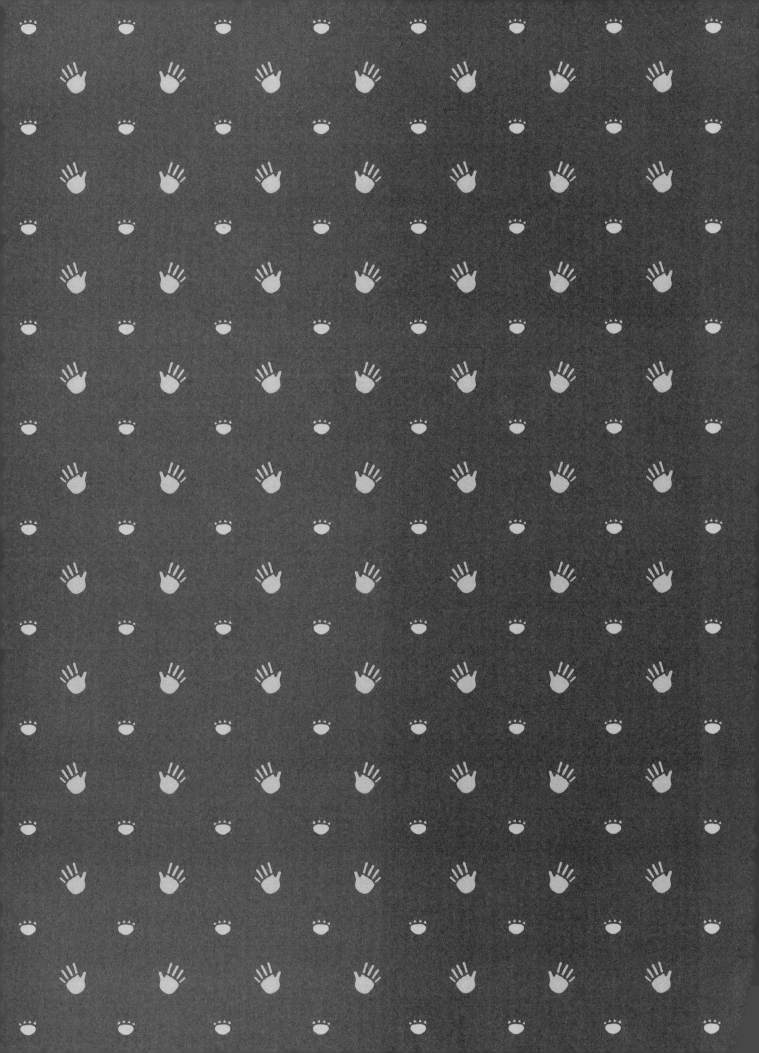